THE THING LOU COULDN'T DO

For Mom and Dad, who always encouraged me to just try

Kids Can Press gratefully acknowledges the financial support of the Government of Ontario, through the Ontario Media Development Corporation; the Ontario Arts Council; the Canada Council for the Arts; and the Government of Canada, through the CBF, for our publishing activity.

Published in Canada and the U.S. by Kids Can Press Ltd.
25 Dockside Drive, Toronto, ON M5A 0B5

Kids Can Press is a Corus Entertainment Inc. company

www.kidscanpress.com

The art in this book was rendered digitally after some procrastination, a fair amount of dawdling and several pep talks.
The text is set in Romp Pro.

Edited by Yasemin Uçar
Designed by Karen Powers

Printed and bound in Shenzhen, China, in 10/2016, through Asia Pacific Offset

CM 17 0 9 8 7 6 5 4 3 2 1

LIBRARY AND ARCHIVES CANADA CATALOGUING IN PUBLICATION

Spires, Ashley, 1978–, author, illustrator
The thing Lou couldn't do / written and illustrated by Ashley Spires.

ISBN 978-1-77138-727-9 (hardback)
I. Title.

PS8637.P57T45 2017 jC813'.6 C2016-903663-4

THE THING LOU COULDN'T DO

Written and illustrated by

ASHLEY SPIRES

KIDS CAN PRESS

This is **LOU**.

Lou and her friends are BRAVE adventurers.

They run FASTER than airplanes.

They build MIGHTY fortresses.

They rescue WILD animals.

Lou is pretty sure
she is going to be a
DEEP-SEA DIVER
when she grows up.

Or a RACE-CAR DRIVER.

Or maybe a PIRATE.

Let's play pirates!
Yeah! We just need a ship.
Up there! The tree can be our ship!
Ummm ...

This is new. Lou has never climbed a tree before.

"It will be an adventure!" says her friend.

Lou loves adventures, but this adventure is UP.
She likes her adventures to be DOWN.

Lou suggests a NOT-UP-A-TREE game.

But her friends have made up their minds.

She'll be there in a minute. She just needs to change her shoes first.

In Captain Lou Skullbuckle's opinion, the couch makes a fantastic pirate ship. But Mom disagrees.

FINE. But her first mate is coming, too.

AHOY!
Land ho!
ARRR, mateys!
They're STILL up there.

Lou tells them that her arm is sore.
And anyway, the cat needs a walk.
Also, she read once that you shouldn't
climb so soon after eating.

There are **SO MANY REASONS** not to try.

I stepped on a slug
this morning. His funeral
is in five minutes.

I just found out I'm part fish and
need water to survive, so if you'll excuse me,
I'll be in the bathtub for the rest of my life.

That asteroid is
headed right for us.
RUN!

My tummy hurts.
I need to sit down.

I CAN'T
climb the tree.

She wishes her friends would just leave her alone. She's FINE down here. Besides, she doesn't even WANT to climb.

What's so great about climbing trees anyway?

The treasure
is THAT WAY!
I can see all the way to
the NORTH POLE
from here!

ARRR!

OH. That does look pretty great.

If only Lou could climb trees.

Meow.
SHOW-OFF.

Maybe she can get up there without climbing! There must be lots of **OTHER WAYS** to get up a tree.

TRAMPOLINE?

POLE VAULT?

HELICOPTER!

SADLY,

helicopters are hard to come by.

It's a call for help.

Shiver me timbers!

Those SCALLYWAGS need a captain ...

It's time for Captain Lou Skullbuckle
to CLIMB ABOARD.

This pirate captain has faced some pretty scary things — sea monsters, hurricanes, even a super-bad brain freeze. And now, Captain Lou Skullbuckle is going to do the scariest thing of all. She's going to CLIMB THIS TREE!

She must be
NEARLY THERE ...

HUH.

THUD!

She knew it.
She CAN'T climb.

NOT YET, anyway.
Purrrrr

She'll be back. Maybe even tomorrow.

After all, Lou loves an adventure.